PERFECTLY POLITE PENGUINS

NOT!

Georgiana Deutsch • Ekaterina Trukhan

LITTLE TIGER

LONDON

Penguins are ALWAYS perfectly polite.

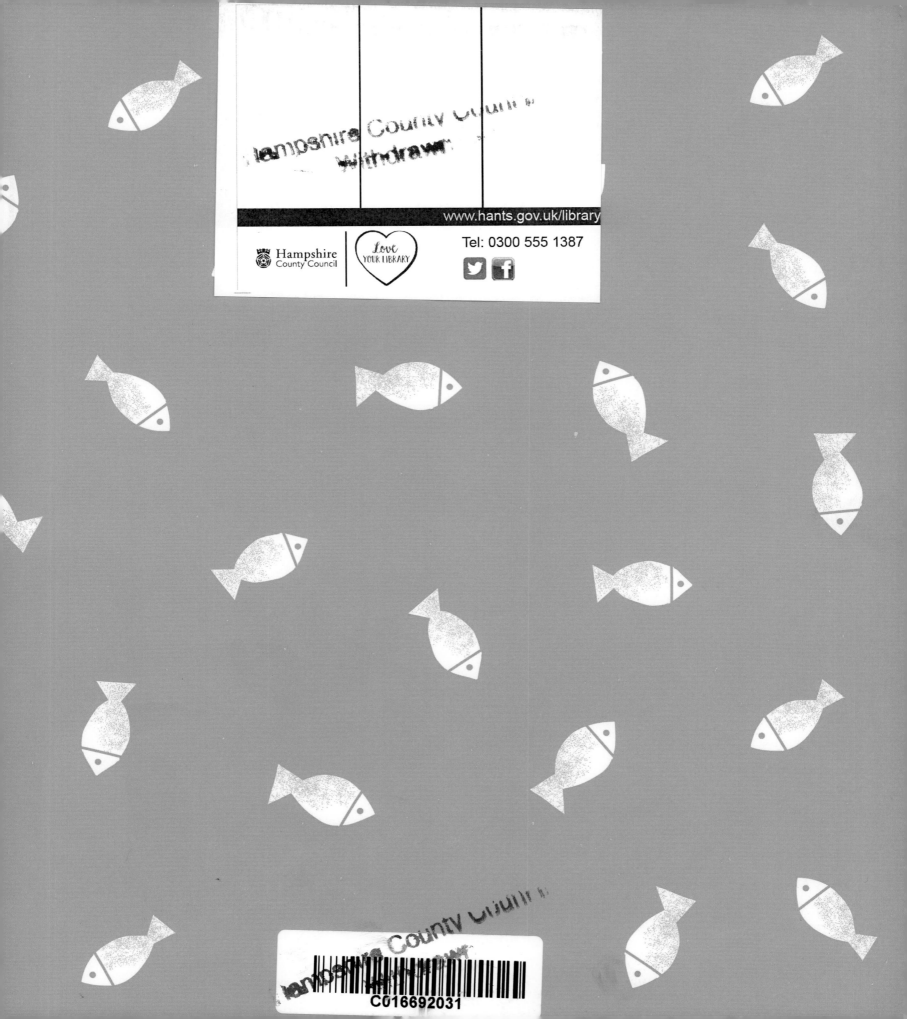

For Freddy, my cheeky little penguin x
- G D

LITTLE TIGER PRESS LTD,
an imprint of the Little Tiger Group
1 Coda Studio, 189 Munster Road, London SW6 6AW
www.littletiger.co.uk

First published in Great Britain 2019
Text by Georgiana Deutsch
Text copyright © Little Tiger Press Ltd 2019
Illustrations copyright © Ekaterina Trukhan 2019
Ekaterina Trukhan has asserted her right to be
identified as the illustrator of this work
under the Copyright, Designs and Patents Act, 1988

A CIP catalogue record for this book is available
from the British Library

All rights reserved · ISBN 978-1-78881-127-9

Printed in China · LTP/1400/2394/0818

10 9 8 7 6 5 4 3 2 1

Penguins always wait their turn.

They love sharing their toys.

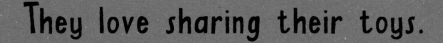

And they NEVER forget to say please and thank you!

Oh, no. Someone's misbehaving again.

This is Polly.
Say hello, Polly!

Polly prefers NOT to be polite.
She says it's . . .

BORING!

Shhhh!

Be quiet, Polly!

We're trying to
listen to the story!

Sometimes Polly interrupts.

Sometimes she forgets to think about how the other penguins might feel.

And she really doesn't like picking up her toys!

At dinnertime, Polly's manners go from bad to worse.
Especially when the penguins have . . .

. . . fishy snacks. Uh oh.

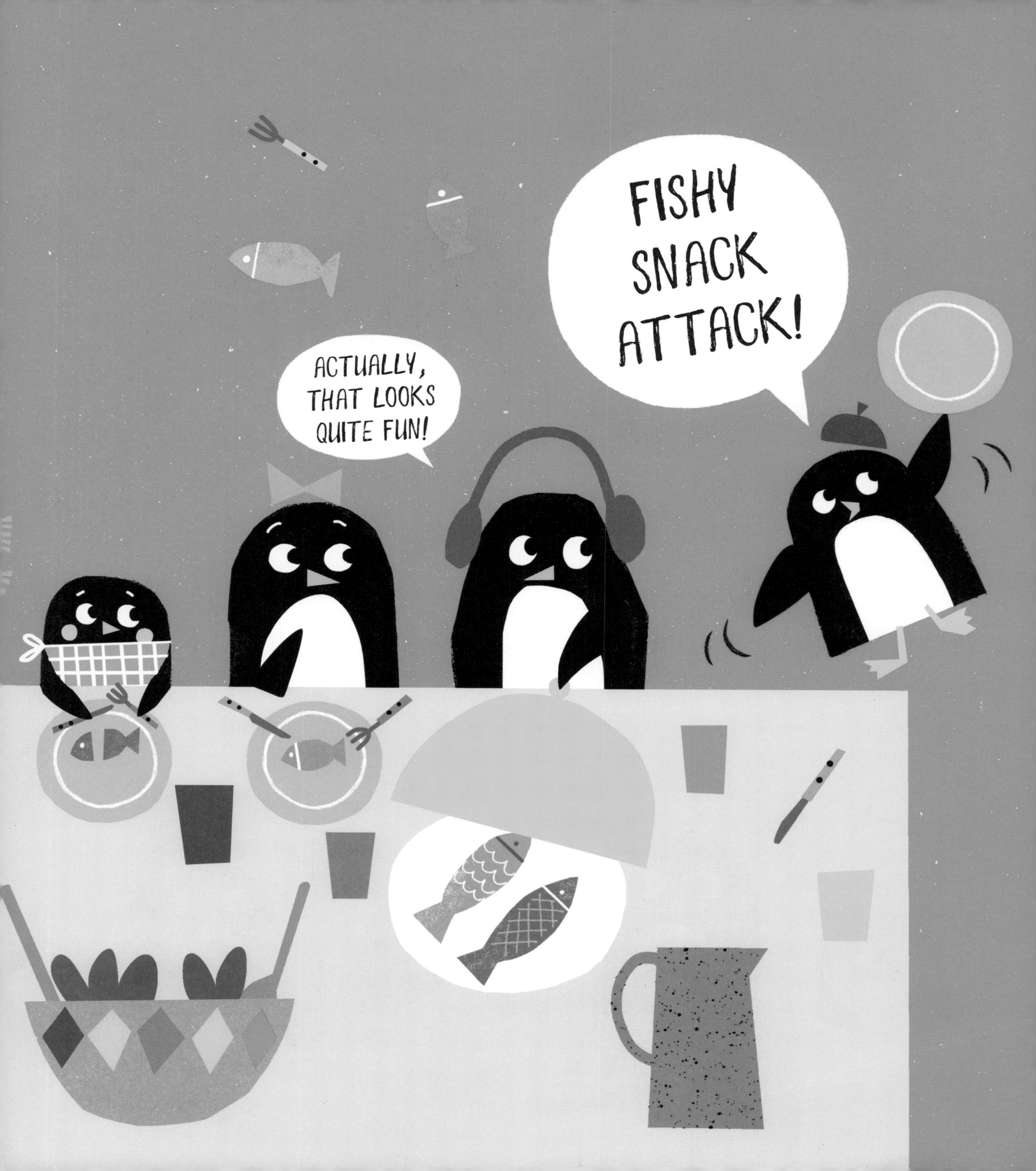
ACTUALLY, THAT LOOKS QUITE FUN!
FISHY SNACK ATTACK!

The perfectly polite penguins don't like it when Polly talks with her mouth full.

When she doesn't use her knife and fork.

And when she grabs the fishy snacks
without asking. Hang on a minute . . .

What's happened to all the perfectly polite penguins?

Oh. Where's Polly going?

Oh dear. Poor baby Peter
doesn't look very happy, does he?

Luckily, Polly knows just how to make
Peter feel better!

Well, that did the trick! Well done, Polly!

Perfectly polite penguins always clear up their toys together.

They always share nicely.

And they always think about how other penguins are feeling.

Even Polly the penguin is perfectly polite!

Well . . .

. . . most of the time!